# BATMAN'S TOP SECRET TOOLS
## A GUIDE TO THE GADGETS

Adapted by Cala Spinner  Illustrated by Patrick Spaziante
Based on the screenplay *Monster Mayhem* written by Heath Corson
Batman created by Bob Kane with Bill Finger

Simon Spotlight
New York  London  Toronto  Sydney  New Delhi

Based on the screenplay by Heath Corson

Copyright © 2016 DC Comics.

BATMAN and all related characters and elements © & ™ DC Comics and Warner Bros. Entertainment Inc. (s16)

SIMON SPOTLIGHT

An imprint of Simon & Schuster Children's Publishing Division

1230 Avenue of the Americas, New York, New York 10020

This Simon Spotlight paperback edition December 2016

All rights reserved, including the right of reproduction in whole or in part in any form.

SIMON SPOTLIGHT and colophon are registered trademarks of Simon & Schuster, Inc.

For information about special discounts for bulk purchases, please contact Simon & Schuster Special Sales at 1-866-506-1949 or business@simonandschuster.com.

Manufactured in the United States of America 1116 LAK

10 9 8 7 6 5 4 3 2 1

ISBN 978-1-4814-7729-1

ISBN 978-1-4814-7730-7 (eBook)

Greetings! My name is Alfred Pennyworth. Welcome to Wayne Manor, home of the brilliant billionaire Bruce Wayne—or, as you might know him, Batman.

Master Wayne has instructed me to give you a tour of the Batcave, his secret headquarters and command center. Are you ready for the tour? Please do come in.

# THE BATCAVE

The Batcave is an essential part of hero work, and as such, its location must be kept secret. Aside from Batman's fellow super heroes, myself, and now you, no one knows where it is.

The Batcave has the most advanced security system in the world, complete with high-tech motion sensors and alarms.

# THE BATCOMPUTER

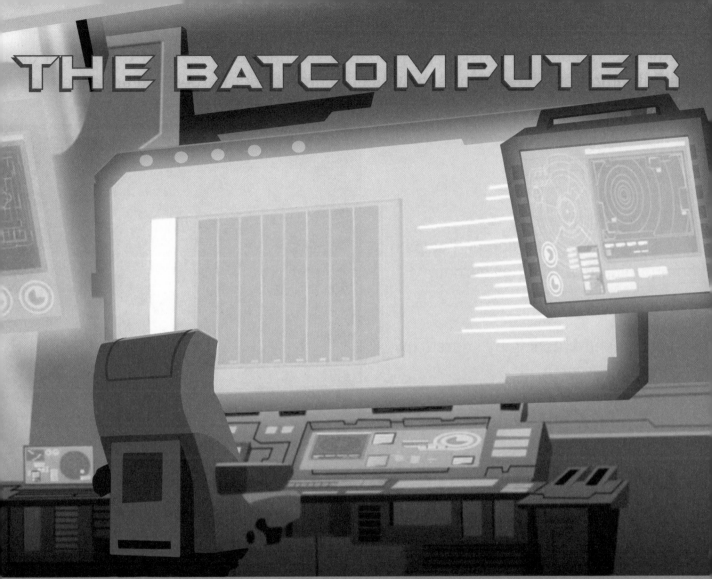

Over here you will find the Batcomputer, specifically made for our Caped Crusader. It is the most highly advanced computer system in Gotham City—and, I daresay, the world.

With its superpowered hard drive, the Batcomputer can analyze data, track crime, synthesize medicines, and keep our heroes knowledgeable about everything going on in Gotham City.

Here you will find armor for Batman and his partner, Red Robin. Sometimes Batman teams up with other heroes too, and you can see images of their armor on the Batcomputer. These high-tech suits both protect our heroes and enhance their special abilities. They also keep their secret identities safe.

## BATSUIT

### COWL

gives Batman night vision and helps him communicate with other heroes.

### CAPE

requires hand-washing by yours truly, Alfred Pennyworth.

## RED ROBIN SUIT

### BATTLE STAFF

is collapsible, making for easy storage on his belt.

# GREEN ARROW SUIT

## QUIVER

keeps arrows secure and ready for action.

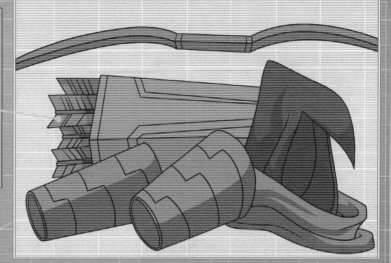

# THE FLASH SUIT

## SPECIAL FRICTION-PROOF MATERIAL

can withstand the speed of the Fastest Man Alive.

# NIGHTWING SUIT

## FLEXIBLE ARMOR

allows Nightwing to use expert acrobatic moves with ease.

# CYBORG

Cyborg also fights crime—but unlike the other super heroes, his armor doesn't come off. Cyborg is half man, half machine.

**BLASTER**
for use in combat

**ENHANCED VISION**
to identify and scan objects

**JET PACK**
used to hover and fly

Of course, there are other benefits to being half machine. With the help of his father, Dr. Silas Stone, Cyborg's abilities can be upgraded with new hardware and software, meaning that he can run faster, fly farther, and fight better as his technology is updated.

# GREEN ARROW'S ARROWS

On the Batcomputer you will see Green Arrow's massive collection of battle arrows. It takes an expert archer to use these tools.

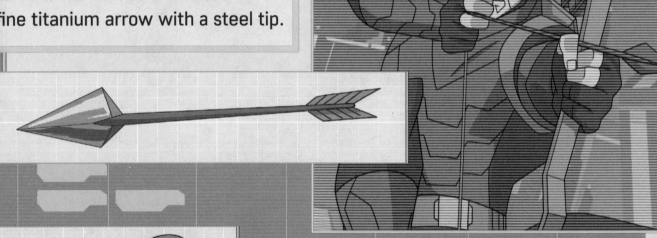

## STANDARD ARROW
A fine titanium arrow with a steel tip.

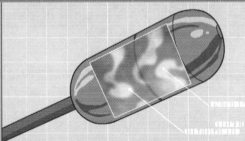

## KNOCKOUT GAS ARROW
This arrow defeats opponents with special knockout gas. It can take down multiple super-villains with only one shot!

## BOXING GLOVE ARROW

Equipped with a boxing glove, this arrow delivers an extra punch.

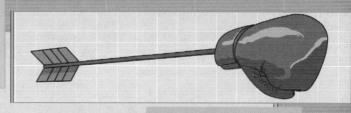

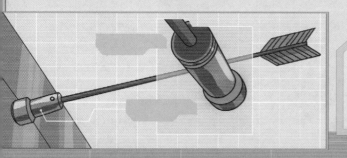

## EXPLOSIVE ARROW

An arrow that blows up on contact with a target.

## SMOKESCREEN ARROW

When fired, this arrow creates a cloud of smoke that is impossible to see through (patent pending).

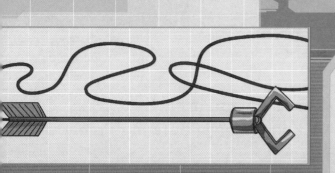

## GRAPPLE ARROW

This arrow anchors itself to surfaces and buildings, allowing Green Arrow to swing off it, similar to Nightwing's Line Launcher.

# UTILITY BELT

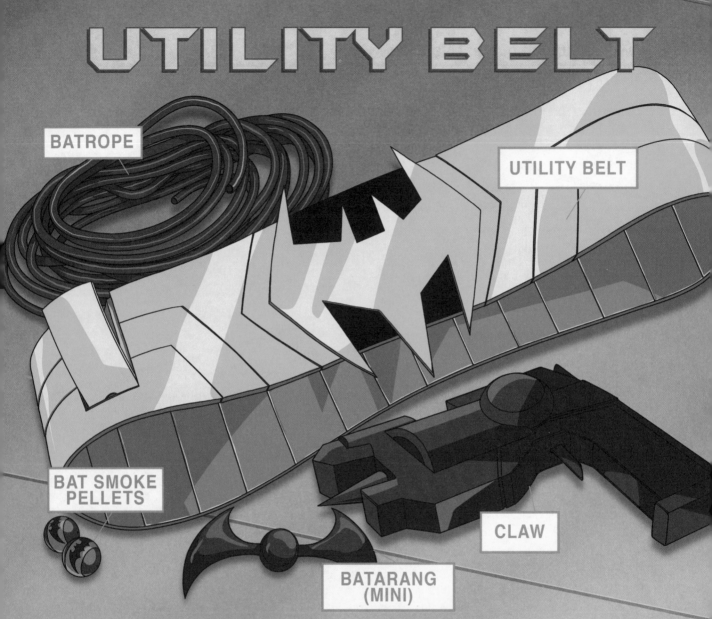

**BATROPE**

**UTILITY BELT**

**BAT SMOKE PELLETS**

**CLAW**

**BATARANG (MINI)**

One of the most important features of Batman's Batsuit is his Utility Belt. Batman's Utility Belt houses the tools our Dark Knight needs to fight crime—trackers, smoke pellets, lasers, and much more.

Let's take a closer look at the tools inside the Utility Belt, shall we?

# STUN DEVICES

Our heroes use Stun Devices to stop criminals and send them running for cover. Efficient and powerful, Stun Devices are useful against Batman's more powerful enemies such as Clayface, Solomon Grundy, and Killer Croc.

# BATARANGS

Tucked inside Batman's Utility Belt are his Batarangs. These slim, bat-shaped boomerangs can slice at vehicle tires, electrify a dangerous device, or be programmed to explode on contact. With their many uses, Batarangs are one of the Dark Knight's favorite gadgets.

# TRACKER

When Batman needs to keep tabs on a suspicious villain, he uses a special device called a tracker. The tracker sends out a signal that helps our heroes find and catch bad guys.

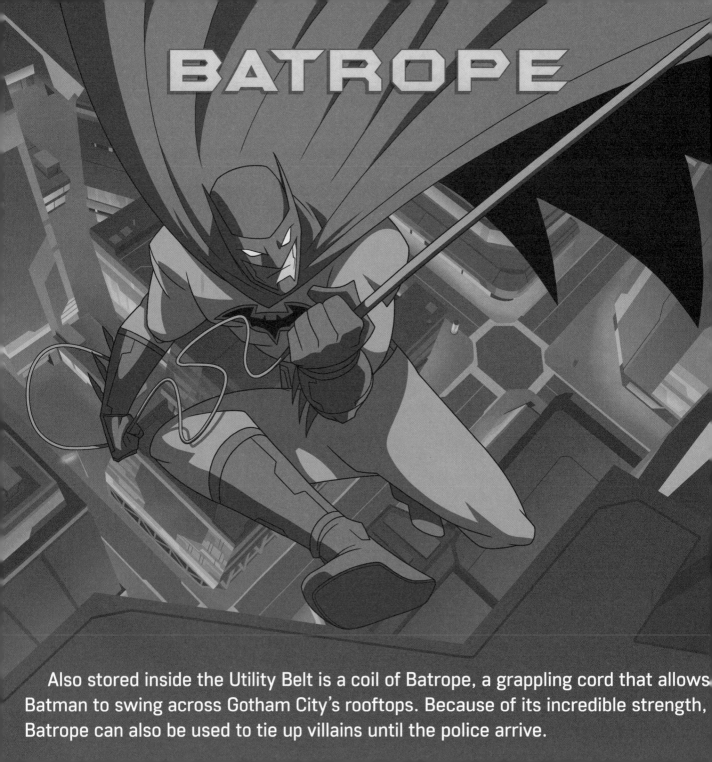

# BATROPE

Also stored inside the Utility Belt is a coil of Batrope, a grappling cord that allows Batman to swing across Gotham City's rooftops. Because of its incredible strength, Batrope can also be used to tie up villains until the police arrive.

# CLAW

Need to grab something that's out of reach fast? Batman's claw is the perfect tool. This useful object can grab hold of anything—and I do mean *anything*—bad guys included.

# NIGHTWING'S TOOLS

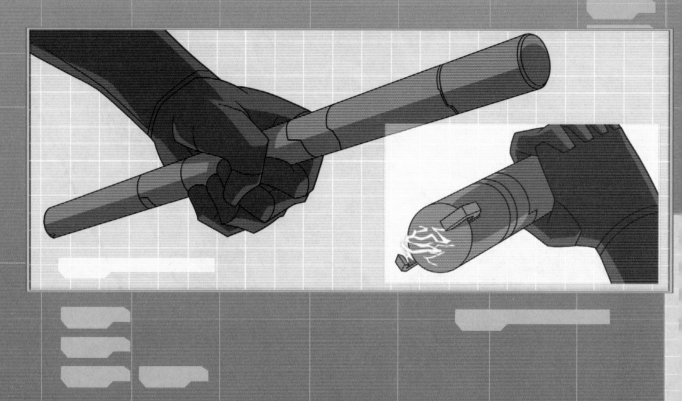

*Zzzap!* These are Nightwing's eskrima sticks, a pair of electric batons used to defeat enemies. Nightwing can also use his eskrima sticks to damage devices, vehicles, and robots by overloading their circuitry with an electric charge.

To your right, you will see Nightwing's line launcher. As a boy, Nightwing trained to be an acrobat. This specialty training prepared him for life as a super hero, using the Line Launcher to get around Gotham City.

In the center of the Batcave you will find the Training Arena. Master Tim—Red Robin—uses this arena to practice his skills in combat.

*Pow!* Today, Master Tim is training against two robots. I hope he doesn't hit them too hard; he tends to make quite a mess during combat training.

# THE BATMOBILE

*Vroom!* The Batmobile is Batman's most useful tool. It's a car that powers itself, drives incredibly fast, and provides a perfect way for Gotham City's Dark Knight to get around. It's also very powerful, with two blaster cannons on the front to fire at Batman's enemies.

A secret ramp helps the Batmobile travel to and from the Batcave undetected. This is our newest version of the car, the sleekest and fastest model yet.

# THE BATWING

The Batwing is Batman's private plane. It was designed with the most cutting-edge technology and flies swiftly through the night sky. The Batwing also has an autopilot feature, meaning that Batman can summon it from the Batcave with just the push of a button.

# THE BAT-GLIDER

For shorter distances, Batman can fly with the help of his Bat-Glider. Although flight is no simple feat, the Bat-Glider is easy to use—when Batman wants to change direction, he moves his body to the side, and the Bat-Glider follows his command.

# CYBER ANIMALS

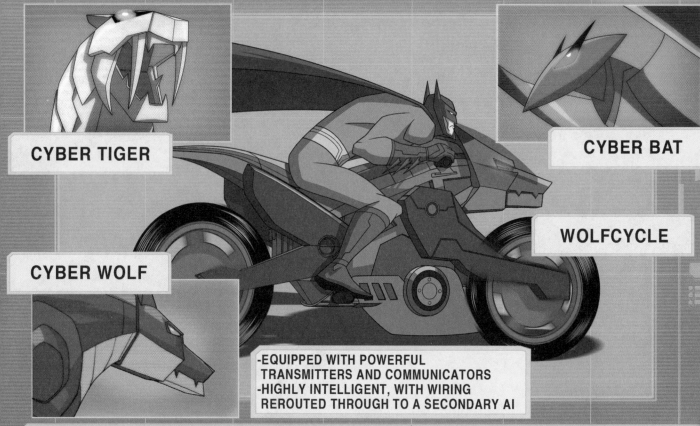

**CYBER TIGER**

**CYBER BAT**

**WOLFCYCLE**

**CYBER WOLF**

-EQUIPPED WITH POWERFUL
TRANSMITTERS AND COMMUNICATORS
-HIGHLY INTELLIGENT, WITH WIRING
REROUTED THROUGH TO A SECONDARY AI

Straight ahead you will meet the Cyber Animals, powerful robots designed by Dr. Kirk Langstrom. These Cyber Animals were originally part of an evil plot to destroy Gotham City, but Dr. Langstrom helped our heroes rewire them for personal use.

The Cyber Animals excel in combat. Their abilities mimic those of animals in the wild—they can bite, pounce, and jump. The Cyber Animals also have special scanners that allow them to analyze and assess potential threats.

# CYBER BAT

can shoot laser beams and becomes a hover board for Red Robin when needed.

# ACE THE CYBER WOLF

transforms into the Wolfcycle, a high-speed motorcycle.

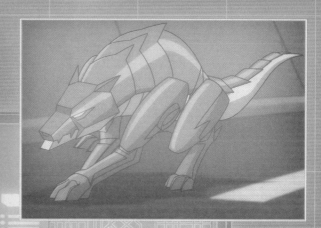

# CYBER TIGER

has a tail that can extend and grab onto higher ledges, allowing for a quick escape.

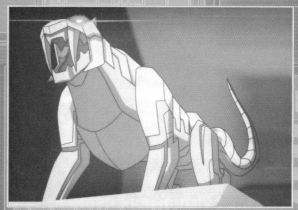

# VIRTUAL REALITY GOGGLES AND GLOVES

Video-game designer Gogo Shoto invented this set of virtual reality goggles and gloves. When one wears them, he or she becomes part of a virtual world. Master Tim trains against virtual opponents using the goggles and gloves from time

# CYBEREX

I saved one of the best tools for last. Are you ready to be impressed? Here, put on the virtual-reality goggles and meet CybeRex!

Batman used CybeRex to defeat the Joker in a virtual-reality battle. CybeRex is a computerized dinosaur with a blaster on its neck, a massive tail, and a powerful

# THE BAT-SIGNAL

I have one final tool to tell you about, one that isn't in the Batcave, but is still important for crime fighting. If you ever need Batman's help, the Bat-Signal is the best way to contact him.

Police Commissioner James Gordon activates the Bat-Signal to get Batman's attention. When Batman sees it, he knows he's needed.

That just about completes our tour of the Batcave. I hope you enjoyed your visit. Do help yourself to some Darjeeling tea and turkey sandwiches on the way out. Please visit again soon, and remember, everything you've seen here is top secret. Batman is counting on you!